THE
BLACK
HORN

A KEEPER'S TALE

J.A. ANDREWS

For those who believe that love and magic are easy to mistake for each other.

PROLOGUE

The bag with the Black Horn bounced against Eliese's back like the prodding of a little sprite, cheering her on to adventure and victory. She raced after her twin brother Rellien, his red curls jouncing wildly as he ran down the goat trail winding high along the cliff. Behind her she could hear Marcus's quick breaths and footsteps. A pebble knocked loose by her foot shot off the side of the path and bounced down the steep slope disappearing into the gorge. The rust-red cliffs stood out in sharp relief against the empty blue sky. Eliese's black hair soaked in the heat from the summer sun, making the top of her head feel like it was too close to a fire.

The bag was lighter than she'd expected. The fabled Black Horn had always looked so grave presiding over the great hall from the mantle. It was a thing of legend, of magic, and though she'd stared at it for hours on end, she'd never before dared to touch it. Until Rellien had set his mind to blowing it and they'd hatched their plan. But now that she'd held it, it felt like...well, it felt like a common ram's horn. A bit big, perhaps,

1

but that was the only difference between it and the horns the watchmen blew.

Still, she couldn't quell the thrill of what they were about to do. Carrying the horn made her feel like some sort of battle maiden fighting valiantly in an ancient tale.

"I think I should blow it first," Marcus called from behind her.

"Why?" Rellien demanded.

"Because I'm older. I'm already twelve."

"Eliese and I will be twelve next month," Rellien objected. "Being barely older doesn't count. I'm blowing the horn because my father is the captain of the keep and some day I will be too." He turned to give Marcus a serious look. "I may have to blow it for real some day."

Marcus opened his mouth to object, but Eliese broke in. "Just let him or he'll argue with you all afternoon."

Marcus scowled from under drooping, sweaty brown locks and kicked a spray of tiny rocks off the thin path, letting them skitter down the slope. But he didn't say anything.

"Lookout Rock!" Rellien declared over his shoulder as they rounded a curve in the cliff face. He clambered off the trail and out onto a huge boulder hanging out over the gorge. "From here we shall see the whole of our fertile land stretched out before us!"

"Fertile?" Eliese asked, looking at the barren cliffs.

"Fine," Rellien said. "Our land rich in ore. And precious metals."

"I'm pretty sure it's just rocky," Marcus said and Eliese giggled.

"And from this, our lofty watchtower," Rellien continued, ignoring them both, "we can spy our enemies from afar!"

Eliese climbed up next to him, the breeze blowing past her

dry and dusty. Far below, the narrow gorge twisted off to the west. At the bottom a thin road plodded along next to a small, parched stream. To the east, the gorge wound up toward the pass at Stone Gap. And at the top of the pass, lodged between the road and the sharp southern cliffs, sat the keep.

"And our great palace." Marcus said with an unenthused sigh. "Also made from ore and precious metals."

"I like it," Eliese came to its defense. "It looks solid. As strong as the cliffs themselves."

"That's because it's made out of the rocks of cliffs themselves," Marcus pointed out.

"It will keep us safe," Eliese insisted, "and that is what it is meant to do."

"Not if a horde of Wildmen come," Rellien said darkly, crouching down and peering west through the canyon. "If wave upon wave of the vicious men come, they'll crash past the keep and spill through onto the plains, ravaging and killing everyone in Queensland."

"That would take a lot of men," Eliese pointed out.

Rellien shrugged. "They're Wildmen. They grow from the grass and rocks. There are countless Wildmen."

"I'm pretty sure Wildmen come from wild women," Eliese said, "not grass and rocks."

Marcus laughed.

"Could you two be more helpful?" Rellien asked, irritated. "You're destroying the moment."

"Right, sorry," Marcus said. He stepped up to the edge of the rock and shaded his eyes and he looked west down the empty gorge. "Captain!" he cried. "The countless hordes approach! And with them come...um...." He looked around for a moment. "...giants! Giants to destroy the walls of the keep."

"The Black Horn, fair lady of Stone Gap!" Rellien cried,

holding out his hand to Eliese. "The army of Wildmen approaches, we need the horn! We need its power! We need it to raise again the legendary army from the very rocks. Indestructible and loyal to only us."

She reached into the sack and wrapped her hand around the horn. Under her fingers the inner curve was smooth as glass. But the outside was rough with ridges like miniature ranges of mountains lined up one after another.

The sunlight sank into the horn, warming the blackness. It called to her for a moment, called to something deep within her, pulling at her gut.

"Fair lady!" Rellien said, wiggling his fingers impatiently at her. "The army approaches!"

Eliese hesitated another moment, but the Black Horn had settled into just a horn. Hollow and lifeless.

"El," Rellien sighed, "You can blow it next. You can be the Queen Lady of the Keep. Have an army of trolls coming. Whatever you want. But you already agreed to let me blow it first."

Eliese stretched the horn out toward her brother.

"Thanks!" he said, grabbing it. "And if you could swoon or something at our impending doom, that would be great."

"I don't swoon." Eliese said, indignant. "I'm perfectly capable of helping solve whatever problems come up. After all, I'm the one who climbed up the mantle to get the horn, and I'm the one who discovered we could get out the watch tower window to reach this goat trail." She scowled at her brother. "Swoon," she muttered.

"Shh!" Rellien whispered, peering down into the empty canyon. "The enemy is right at our feet! It is time!"

Rellien held the horn for a moment, then glanced at Eliese and Marcus. The three of them stood perfectly still.

Eliese's heart quickened. Her brother lifted the horn up and it looked too dark against the sky, too black. Marcus stepped close to Eliese, his shoulder up against hers.

"What if it works?" he whispered, his voice barely audible. "What if we raise an army?"

Eliese opened her mouth to tell him it wasn't possible, but her mouth felt too dry to talk. She leaned against him, suddenly frightened of the horn. Rellien brought the horn to his lips and drew in a breath. Eliese grabbed Marcus's hand and squeezed, drawing back. Rellien blew out a great burst of air.

And out of the horn came a weak honk.

Like a goose. Coughing.

There was a breath of silence before Eliese's fear rushed out of her in a laugh and the boys joined in.

"Blow it again!" Marcus called.

Rellien did, and this time the honk ended in a squeak.

Their laughter echoed off the canyon walls.

"My turn!" Eliese said, reaching out for it.

She took the horn from her brother. It felt warm, but...vacant. She set her lips against the unyielding opening and taking a deep breath, blew as hard as she could.

The horn let out a sickly warble. The boys fell into gales of laughter, but Eliese didn't join them. Against her hand, the horn hummed. And something in her gut stirred, as though the surface of a deep pool had been disturbed.

The laughter of her brother and Marcus turned to great war cries and their voices rang out, the noise doubling and tripling back on them until the entire canyon was full of it.

Eliese closed her eyes. The horn felt alive and restless in her hands, and the something inside her reached for it, longing for...what, she wasn't sure.

5

The boys' yells echoed loud and wild, filling the air and crashing against the cliffs until the ground beneath her feet trembled and her eyes snapped open. Marcus and Rellien were jumping and hollering near the edge, but the rock was shaking with more than that. She turned to look up the slope above them. The rocks were moving, rushing toward them like a river of stone.

She cried out to the boys and grabbed for them, pulling them down and huddling together as the stream of rocks rushed down the mountain, crashing down only an arm's reach past the rock they were on. Eliese clutched the horn to her chest, feeling its warmth and that strange calling again.

They clung together for a half dozen breaths while the sound of the rockslide faded down the cliff. Peering over the edge they saw the thin, light path of the avalanche leading straight down to a pile of rock on the gorge floor.

Silence reigned over the canyon.

"Maybe it's time to head back," Rellien whispered, the words shaky.

"Agreed," Marcus said quickly.

The two turned back toward the goat trail, their eyes wild and wary. Eliese placed the Black Horn back into her bag.

"So much for the legend of the Black Horn," Rellien whispered with an unsteady grin as he passed her.

Eliese forced a smile at him, disappointment and uncertainty swirling through her. She let her fingers linger on the horn for an extra breath, but the horn sat silent and empty.

"So much for the legend," she answered slowly.

But the boys were already dashing ahead on the path toward home.

1

TEA WITH A KEEPER
SEVEN YEARS LATER.

Eliese hung the kettle over the fire and turned toward the table in the great hall where Keeper Oriana leaned back in her chair. The curly red head of her twin brother Rellien and Marcus's brown mop leaned over a dice game at the far end.

"Is the king as bad off as we hear?" Eliese asked, hoping the question wasn't impertinent, and hoping her voice didn't sound as nervous as she felt. Eliese's father had been a child the last time a Keeper had come to Stone Gap. There were only ever a few of them in Queensland. As preservers of knowledge and history, and wielders of magic, the Keepers stayed at court to advise rulers or witnessed and recorded the most crucial events in the land.

The fact that one was here at Stone Gap made Eliese's gut turn to stone. No one this important ever made it all the way here, to the edges of the civilized land unless there was something truly perilous happening.

Oriana nodded. "His mind wanders and his body weakens." Her hair was long and almost completely grey, but there was an alertness about her face that kept her from looking old.

"But the king is so young," Eliese said, setting out tea cups and a teapot. The king was barely older than herself.

"Too young. It began as a hunting injury, but has turned into a dreadful illness. And with no heir, the last thing this disaster of a succession needs is a warlord like Noreth invading."

Eliese's heart clenched at the name, the fear that had sat in her gut for weeks rising up again. The Wildmen had lived on the edge of Queensland for as long as anyone could remember, skirmishing with them. Occasionally attacking in force. A generation ago, in an attempt to establish peace, the last king's cousin married the Wildmen's war chief. And for a time it worked. Until their son, Noreth grew into power. Now his connection to Queensland didn't lead him toward peace, it gave him hopes of attaining the throne. As the present king lay dying, families with royal blood all across the country were angling for the throne, creating alliances. And in two days, Noreth would be here with an army of ten thousand to stake his claim. "Will the reinforcements from the king reach us before he does?"

The dice game stilled as both Rellien and Marcus listened for her answer.

Oriana paused. "I'm not sure."

"They have to come," Eliese said, clutching a cup in her hand so tightly that the ridge along the bottom dug into her palm. "We're a small garrison. We've enough men to keep the bandits in the hills under control, but we're not equipped to stop an army!"

"We'll stop anything that comes through the gap," Rellien

said. "The keep is well positioned and no matter how large the army is, they still have to come through the pass a few at a time."

"But they will just keep coming," Eliese said. "They'll exhaust us and kill us and then nothing will stop them from reaching the plains."

"We just need to hold them off until the king's army gets here, El," Rellien said.

"How can you be so calm?" Eliese demanded, thrusting aside a lock of black hair that had fallen in her face. "We don't even know when Noreth will get here. We've had another whole day of this blasted fog, which is never going to lift, none of our scouts have returned--" Eliese shut her mouth, trying to quell the fear that ate at her. It didn't matter how close the reinforcements were. The sixty men stationed at Stone Gap couldn't hold the road against Noreth's force of Wildmen, even for half a day. They'd be slaughtered.

"We might not be enough," Marcus said quietly. "But we have to try."

She turned away from them and looked out the window, wishing she could see through the thick fog that had sat in the gorge for days. But the evening outside was a dreary haze.

Bread and cold meat were brought in and Rellien, Marcus, and Oriana served themselves. Eliese forced herself to put some food on her plate.

"I don't suppose the king's army is bringing with it a dragon," she asked Oriana, "Or some great magical talisman that can defeat an approaching horde?"

Oriana gave a small smile. "When I first became a Keeper, I thought magic could fix anything. In theory, there could be magic strong enough to stop an army, but practically speaking, it's impossible. It would cost too much." She shook her head. "Magic always has a price."

Eliese fidgeted with a piece of bread. "Always?"

She waited for the Keeper to offer a quick nod, brushing off the question. But the woman looked at Eliese for a long, thoughtful moment.

"All the magic I've ever heard of does. What you call magic, the Keepers call energy. And it can be manipulated. For instance I can draw heat from the fire, and put it in the kettle." She paused a moment and the kettle over the fire began to hiss as the water inside of it boiled.

Eliese glanced at Marcus and Rellien and saw their eyes wide, staring at the boiling kettle.

Oriana winced and rubbed her hands together. "But moving the energy...hurts."

"I've heard that." Eliese pulled the boiling kettle off the fire and poured the water into the teapot, watching it steam in wonder. It should have taken at least three or four more minutes to boil the water. "And if you tried to do too much magic..."

"It would kill me." Oriana looked into the fire. "Heating the kettle causes a little discomfort. But doing something strong enough to stop an army? There's certainly no one alive who could wield that sort of power and survive."

"What we need," Rellien said, grinning, "is the Black Horn."

Eliese started at the mention of the horn. She'd thought of almost nothing else for days. She looked up at it, sitting still in its place on the mantle. Her dreams had been haunted by it and her waking hours spent wishing the legends about it were real. Twice, when she'd been alone in the great hall, she'd almost picked it up, remembering the way it had pulled at her so many years ago, the way it had hummed against her hand.

"Is that it?" Oriana said, peering up at the horn. "I've heard the legend of the horn."

"So have we," Marcus laughed. "But it turns out it's just a horn."

Eliese measured tea leaves into the first two cups.

"And not even a good horn," Rellien added. "If you want to find anything magic around here, you'd be better off looking in Eliese's tea."

Eliese's hand froze and she shot him a scowl. How dare he bring this up in front of a Keeper? Joking about it among the family was one thing, but this...

She braced for a laugh from Oriana, but the Keeper turned to her, interested.

"Is your tea magical?"

"No," Eliese said.

"Maybe," Rellien said at the same time. Next to him Marcus nodded.

"It's just tea!" Eliese said.

And it was just tea. Usually. Although sometimes she was almost positive it wasn't. But whatever went on during those times wasn't anything she could explain. Or even anything she was sure actually happened. It certainly wasn't something she wanted to claim in front of a Keeper who actually could do magic.

"Why do they think it's magical?" Oriana asked.

Eliese shot her brother and Marcus a black look. "Sometimes if my father is having trouble sleeping, my tea helps him. But it's just the tea."

Rellien shook his head. "It might be more than that. If there's something Eliese wants from you, or for you. If she brews you some tea and you drink it, well, the thing...sort of...happens."

"It's just coincidence," Eliese said. "Marcus, tell her."

Marcus grinned at her. "It might be coincidence. But if you were mad, there's no way I'd drink tea you poured for me."

Eliese glared at him and pointedly poured water into one of the cups. The tea leaves swirled, staining the water a thin green. She leaned across the table and placed it in front of him. "Like this?"

Marcus eyebrows raised and he leaned back away from the cup. "Did I mention how lovely you look today?"

There was a scuffle under the table and a thunk. Marcus grunted in pain and grabbed his leg, giving Rellien a black look.

"That's my sister," Rellien said, "and she does not look lovely."

Eliese raised one eyebrow. She poured water into the second cup, leaned over the table, and set it firmly in front of Rellien. Her brother looked at her for a moment, then slid the cup away with one finger. "I mean, you are a vision. And I'm not thirsty."

"It's just tea." Eliese laughed, turning back to Oriana. "Would you like some?"

The Keeper studied Eliese for a long moment. She glanced back at the men, neither of whom had taken a drink. "Your mother was from a foreign land, was she not? I have heard that you take after her."

Eliese nodded and pushed her thick black hair over her shoulder, self-consciously. "My father met her on a island in the Southern Sea and she came back as his wife. She died when Rellien and I were born, but the people of Stone Gap say that they'd never seen a man so smitten as my father, that my mother bewitched him. But everyone agrees they were happy."

12

Eliese paused. "She became a sort of...talisman to the keep. They would come to her to be blessed. She always did what she could to help him in their troubles and the people said her touch was charmed. But she never claimed it was magic."

Oriana looked at the teapot for a long moment, then met Eliese's gaze. "Do you think you brew magic tea?"

There was no mockery in the question, and its sincerity caught Eliese off guard. The honesty of the question made her feel...anchored. Made whatever it was within herself feel more real.

"I don't know. I know when I want something..." She looked at the Keeper, trying to put it into words. How could she explain the...whatever it was that she could find sometimes, deep within herself. The hidden well that she could dip into and splash out just the tiniest bit, somehow infuse it into the tea. "'Want' isn't a strong enough word. When I'm *desperate* for something while I brew tea...sometimes it happens." She paused, thinking about how mundane the results always were. "Although it's never anything that can't be explained another way.

"I love my father, and...sometimes I think he just feels that. And it calms him."

Oriana smiled. "It's astonishing how often love and magic are mistaken for each other." She considered Eliese for a moment. "Does it tire you? Or hurt you to brew it?"

Eliese shook her head. "It doesn't hurt."

"But she sleeps like the dead that night," Rellien said. "If she sleeps past dawn we know she's been up brewin'."

Eliese pressed her lips together, but said nothing. It was true. When it worked, when she could find that deep place inside of her, those nights she could barely get up to bed before falling asleep. She searched the Keeper's face for something, some sign of what she was thinking. It sounded stupid saying it out loud. "But it's not actually magic. It's just tea."

Oriana considered her for another long moment. "Brew me some."

Eliese laughed. "It won't work. I don't want anything from you."

"Nothing at all?"

Of course there was something. The worry that had gnawed at her for a fortnight shoved its way to the surface. This was a Keeper. Here. In Stone Gap.

Eliese set the teapot down and took Oriana's cup. She picked out some tea leaves and set them gently in the bottom of the cup. Then she let her worry rise, let the fear that she'd been carrying lift up to the surface, opening something up. And there it was, the deep pool filled with yearning and want. She tipped the teapot over the cup and poured out the hot water, adding to it her longing, dripping it out in drops of fierce desire.

"I want the men of the keep to be safe," she whispered, handing Oriana the cup.

Oriana took the cup and held it before her face, looking into it for a long moment before taking a drink. She closed her eyes, sitting very still. Eliese watched her, barely breathing.

"Do you not wish for your own safety?" Oriana asked, finally looking up.

Eliese let out a short laugh. "I am always safe behind these walls." She shot another glare at her brother and Marcus. "We could all stay safe behind these walls. It is those who would leave to fight that need to worry."

"The tea is delicious." Oriana took another drink. "And I

have no idea if it is magical. I feel...something. But it may all be because I'm looking to."

Eliese nodded. "That is what I tell my father." *And myself.* "It's just tea."

"Hmmm," Oriana said noncommittally. "Perhaps." She glanced up at the mantle. "Would you mind if I looked at the horn?"

The foggy day left the room gloomy, and on the mantle the black ram's horn sat like a curl of blackness, darker than the shadows. Eliese reached up, her hand hesitating only a moment before picking it up. It felt like nothing other than a hollow horn. When she handed it to Oriana, the woman's hands looked thin and pale against it.

"Tell me the legend as you know it," Oriana said quietly, turning the horn over in her hands.

"When the mason's were building this keep," Eliese gestured to the walls around her, "before they had completed the outer wall, the Wildmen of the west came with their vicious war bands. With no protection from the approaching death, the people fled. The last to leave were a mason named Kellen and his younger brother Tann, whose legs were weak.

"Before the two could leave, Kellen was bitten by a rock snake. Kellen wouldn't survive the journey home and Tann didn't have the strength to flee on his own. The brothers knew they were doomed. But an old healer woman appeared as if by magic. She closed herself in a room with Kellen. When she emerged, Kellen had died and she held this Black Horn.

"'Your brother's final gift,' she said, handing the horn to Tann. 'His strength for you when you need it.' Then the woman disappeared.

"Tann got himself to the front of the keep. Below the bands

15

of the Wildmen were winding closer along the bottom of the gorge like a stream of poison water.

"He lifted the horn to his lips, and blew with all his grief and fear and fury." Eliese paused. "And an army arose from the very rocks of the gorge. An army of warriors with Kellen's face, indestructible as stone. They swept down on the Wildmen and crushed them."

Oriana raised an eyebrow. "That would be handy about now." She ran her hands over the black ridges, then closed her eyes and bowed her head over it. Eliese watched for something. Anything. The Black Horn lay still and lifeless in the woman's hands.

Oriana looked up, her brow knit. "It holds no power," she said finally.

Eliese felt something within her sink.

"It holds no ability to make a horn call either," Marcus said. "It's the worst horn I've ever heard."

Oriana smiled. "I didn't mean it didn't have the ability to hold power, just that it's empty of power right now. Or it was, until I put some into it." She looked at the horn for a long moment. "It is holding that. It has an echo. A memory of...purpose." She shook her head. "But it's empty. And the emptiness feels very, very old.

"If it did once raise an army from the rocks, it doesn't have that power to any longer."

"Can you fill it?" Eliese asks quietly.

Oriana shook her head. "The amount of power this can hold is vast. Far more than I could supply." She looked at Eliese sympathetically. "If I were to try to fill it, it would kill me. And even then, I don't think it would raise an army. It's empty of more than just energy. It would need a spell to use that energy and turn stones into an army. Honestly, I don't even know if that's possible. If it were filled, it would just be a horn, holding a lot of power. And doing nothing else."

She stood and handed the horn back to Eliese. "But don't lose hope. There may not be armies of stone coming to your aid, but there is an army of men. More than enough to hold the Gap against any size army that Noreth can bring."

Marcus and Rellien rose too and walked with the Keeper toward the door while Eliese put the Black Horn back on the mantle. It was so light she could have lifted it with a finger.

"I will send a raven to the army, urging them to hurry." Oriana paused at the door. "And I can't fail."

Eliese turned to find the Keeper smiling warmly at her.

"You made me tea and wished for me to keep your family safe. How can I do otherwise?"

Eliese forced a small smile. The others left and she sank back down into her chair. The Black Horn sat on the mantle looking smaller and less black than it ever had. The worry that had taken up residence in her gut flared to life like a fire, burning her stomach.

She set some leaves into her own cup, picked up the teapot, and paused for a moment.

"I want my family safe," she whispered. The longing rushed through her, filling her chest like a surge of water rising from that deep, primal place. "I want my home safe. I want no enemy to come near."

She tilted the pot and the water poured into her cup, a smooth river catching the silver, foggy light from the window. Dipping into the well of emotion within her, she added her longing to the water. She set the pot down and picked up the cup. Her hand shook, sending ripples across the surface. She closed her eyes and took a drink.

The teapot had gone cold and a rush of tepid water flooded

her mouth. It was so weak it tasted like tainted water instead of tea. Thin but sharp, and it cut through her mouth and sank down into her, slicing through any small hope that had grown.

Anger at the approaching army and the slow reinforcements and the useless tea surged up like a burning flood.

Eliese took the cup and hurled it into the fire.

2

THE OFFER

The evening dragged on interminably. The tea and the food had been cleared away, but Eliese couldn't bring herself to go up to her room. It felt too distant and lonely. She wanted to be here, in the heart of the keep, with the quiet bustle of activity always within earshot. Sitting in one of the tall chairs near the hearth, she stared into the fire, willing herself to think of anything besides the approaching army.

Marcus appeared after a while, dropping down into a chair next to her and stretching his feet out toward the fire. She waited for him to speak, to say something that would make her smile, but he stayed silent.

For a long stretch the only sound in the room was the cracking of the fire. Eliese's thoughts tumbled around each other. Fear of the fighting that was drawing ever closer to her home, thoughts of Marcus, her brother, her father lying dead on the rocky floor of the gorge, Noreth's army flowing past Stone Gap unhindered. Flashes of memory of Rellien and

Marcus as children, grinning, laughing, running off to do something reckless.

She closed her eyes and took deep breath, trying to control the dread that was rising in her.

There was a rustle and Marcus's hand closed over hers. Her eyes snapped open and she found him staring up onto the mantle, his hand gripping hers tightly.

"It's a shame the horn doesn't work," he said.

His hand felt warm around hers and she hoped he couldn't feel her terror. Eliese followed his gaze up to the mantle. The Black Horn sat crooked on its stand where she'd put it earlier. It looked off-balance, precarious.

"Yes it is."

Silence fell between them again

"When the fighting comes," he began.

Eliese squeezed his hand. "Please don't," she whispered. "I can't bear to think about it."

"Next year," he began again, glancing at her for just a heartbeat before looking back at the fire, "when the position of watch captain opens, I planned on asking your father for it."

Eliese turned toward him, the coming battle momentarily forgotten. "That's a brilliant idea! You should be watch captain. The men already follow you. There's no better choice in the keep."

He gave her a tight smile. "I've been trying. I've been joining Rellien in his strategy lessons and when Rellien is captain of the keep, I think I could help him..."

Eliese shifted in her chair, resolutely shoving aside the voice that told her that it was foolish to discuss any future past the next few days. She felt a surge of happiness at the idea of Marcus getting a position of such regard. "My brother will need you," she said. "He's so focused on what could be that he loses sight of what actually is. You've always brought him back down to earth."

Marcus shifted in his chair, keeping his focus on their clasped hands. "Yes, I want to help your brother. And help the keep. But..." He glanced up at her. "...it's also the only position in the keep that your father might approve of as a possible match for his daughter."

Something breathtaking and vaguely painful clamped down in Eliese's chest and she opened her mouth to say something, but Marcus hurried on.

"I know this isn't the right time to say this, and I don't need you to tell me what you think of the idea, I just—Noreth will be here in two days and I don't know if I'll—" He clenched his mouth shut for a moment. "I just wanted to make sure you knew."

The tangle of emotions in Eliese was too much to decipher, but underneath it all ran a deep rightness. Marcus's face had never looked so frightened. She reached over until she held his hand in both of hers.

"Please still be here in a year," she whispered. "Promise me you'll tell me this again in a year."

He opened his mouth to say something when footsteps rang out from the hallway.

"Marcus!" Rellien's voice called out.

With a last squeeze of Eliese's hand, Marcus stood and walked toward the door. Rellien burst into the great hall.

"My father's called a council. One of our scouts has returned. Noreth will be here by dawn."

3

THE COUNCIL

"He'll be here at dawn?" Eliese rose out of her chair as her panic flared. "How could he possibly be here this quickly?"

"He must have pushed his troops as fast as they could go while the fog held. It's probably he knows that our reinforcements aren't here yet."

Eliese took a step toward him. "What are we going to do?"

"Father's considering what terms to offer Noreth."

"Terms?" Her voice sounded shrill. She looked at Marcus, but found his face unreadable. "Noreth will never agree to terms. He wants himself set up as king. Nothing else we offer him will be enough. He doesn't want terms, he wants us dead."

"No one expects him to agree to them, El," Rellien said tiredly, rubbing his hands across his face. "But maybe it will give us a little time before we need to actually face him."

Eliese's mind crashed up against the idea like a wave on an immovable cliff. "You can't face him before we have reinforcements. The garrison couldn't hold the pass against an army of Wildmen, even for an hour. You'd be slaughtered."

"Thanks for the vote of confidence," Rellien said dryly. "You know we can't sit here and do nothing. If Noreth gets past the keep he'll be on the plains and a battle there will be a massacre for both sides." He gave a heavy sigh. "Everyone but you has already accepted that this was coming."

"Please don't do this," she grabbed at his arm. "There must be something else."

He leaned forward and kissed her on the forehead. "There's no time for other options." He disengaged her hand from his sleeve. "Marcus, the council is starting." Without another glance at her, he strode out of the room.

Eliese followed after them, straight into the council room.

Her father Captain Joran, Keeper Oriana, and several others were bent over a map, discussing things quietly. When Joran caught sight of her, his brow creased. She wasn't officially part of the council, but she crossed her arms and raised her chin. With a disapproving frown, Joran turned back to the map. But he didn't tell her to leave. She grabbed a chair between Marcus and Rellien.

"We have multiple confirmations now," Captain Joran said to the room. "Noreth will reach the gorge during the night. He must have pushed his troops hard to get here so quickly, so they will be tired. But if he did that, we must assume he knows that our reinforcements aren't here yet.

"We'll parley to offer terms." Joran looked around the room. "But unless someone can come up with terms that Noreth would actually accept, I don't think we can hope to put off the battle for more than a few hours.

"The reinforcements won't be here before late tomorrow night. And even that might be optimistic." Joran ran his hands through his hair. "So if anyone has ideas of anything we can offer Noreth that he'd at least be willing to consider, or any ideas how a battalion of sixty men can hold the pass against an army of ten thousand, I would love to hear it."

The council offered half-hearted ideas, but there was nothing that a small keep in a rocky gorge had to offer a man who wanted nothing more than conquest.

Eliese looked around the room, her heart sinking. There was nothing they could do. All these men were going to be killed in a doomed effort to hold the pass.

Beside her, Marcus's hand sat on his leg, his knee bouncing nervously. She thought of how it had felt, holding her own. How the idea of marrying him, of the future they could have had felt so full and good and right.

She felt a surge of warmth at the thought that he'd planned so much to marry her. It was an odd feeling, this realization that she had something, that she *was* something that someone would value that much.

And Noreth wanted to take it all, not because he hated her, just because she and her world stood in his way.

If only she had something Noreth would value that much.

The answer sprang into her mind and clamped around her heart. For a moment she couldn't breathe. She put her hands in her lap and clasped them together so no one could see them trembling.

It was the only way. But Noreth was a horrible, vicious man. The stories of the things he'd done to people...

She looked at her hands, clenched together. What she wanted was Marcus's hand back around hers. She wanted something to keep everything she loved safe. But what if that something was her?

This was the way to stop Noreth, and no one could offer it

but her. She took a deep breath and prayed that her voice wouldn't shake. At the next lull in the conversation, she leaned forward.

"Offer me."

The room went silent and every face turned toward her.

"Noreth is looking for a wife," she continued. "He thinks it will give him a legitimate shot at the throne. Offer me. We're a noble family, the King is a cousin—"

"No," both Rellien and Markus said flatly.

Her father's face darkened. "Absolutely not."

"It's an offer he would at least consider," Eliese pointed out, her heart pounding both from fear of the idea, and from anger at being dismissed. "The best offer that anyone in this room has suggested."

"It is," Joran answered.

"It might actually buy us some time—" Eliese stopped short at her father's unexpected agreement.

"And if we'd tried sooner it might have even worked." He looked at Eliese and smiled sadly. "Not that I ever would have let that man near you. But it doesn't matter any longer. We've also received word that Noreth has agreed to a marriage with Lady Sielan."

The room sat silent for a breath, in shock before it erupted in talk. Lady Sielan was devious, constantly vying for power. She was also one of the closer cousins to the king.

"Peace," Captain Joran said, and the room quieted reluctantly.

"But if he's allied with her," Eliese said, a spark of hope flaring, "won't he call off his attack? He can't invade a country he's trying to ally with."

Her father glanced over at Keeper Oriana.

She shook her head. "I don't believe he'll call off the attack.

He has no reason to. The country is in such disarray at the moment that it might splinter into duchies at the slightest pressure. Noreth isn't a man to shy away from such an opportunity. If his invasion succeeds, he'll gain a great deal of power. If not, he'll cash in on his alliance with Lady Sielan. If his troops strengthen her own, there isn't much in Queensland that could stop them. Both he and Lady Sielan are clever and ambitious enough to see an opportunity like this and seize it." She looked around the room. "I don't see any way to stop the attack now."

Eliese shrank back in her chair. Marcus sat stiffly beside her and Rellien dropped his head down into his hands. The room was silent until Captain Joran cleared his throat.

"Well, then, if there is a fight coming, let us plan our part."

Someone spread a map of the gorge out across the table and the men stood to look at it. Eliese hesitated for a moment, but she couldn't sit there and listen to them plan their deaths. She slipped out of her chair and fled from the room.

4

AN ARMY OF STONE

Eliese had meant to go to her room, but she found herself instead in the great hall, sinking back into her chair by the fire. The world outside had fallen into darkness and the corners of the hall were full of shadows.

A wave of exhaustion swept over her and she leaned back in the chair, her body feeling too heavy to move. A small laugh escaped her when she realized she'd brewed tea twice today— once for Oriana and once for herself. The fire burned lower and the shadows slipped closer. Feeling cold and small, Eliese closed her eyes.

When she opened them again, the fire had burned down into dark coals breathing out only occasional deep red light. She sat up straight, looking out the window, her heart terrified that she'd see the light of dawn creeping across the sky. But the world still lay in blackness.

She sank back, covering her face with shaking hands. She had to stop it. If the men of the keep went out to hold the road, Noreth's army would ride through them like grass. Fear coursed through her, filling her stomach with a roiling mass of dread. She shoved herself out of the chair, pacing back and forth before the coals.

There had to be *something* that could be done. Something to stop the army. She wanted to transform into a dragon and attack. She wanted to wipe the army away with a great wind. Tear up a mountain and throw it into their path.

Turning back toward the mantle, her gaze caught on the spiral of darkness of the Black Horn. She strode over to it and snatched it off the mantle. Her fingers wrapped around it and the horn felt rough and cold against her skin.

It didn't matter that it was useless. It didn't matter that the horn wasn't real. She had dreamed of the powers it held for years, and the hope was too ingrained in her to do anything else.

She raised it to her lips and blew.

A long, rich note rang out of the horn, thrumming against Eliese's hands and filling the room with a wave of sound. Even the stones beneath her feet vibrated.

Eliese yanked the horn away from her mouth and stared at it.

She lifted it again and blew. This time the note was thinner. A third blow made barely any noise at all.

Eliese stared at the horn for a long moment, her mind racing.

It was Keeper Oriana. She'd put some magic, some energy into the horn.

Eliese closed her eyes and focused her mind on the horn. For a long moment it felt thin and still and lifeless in her hands. Until it felt like more. There was a depth to it, a hollowness. She breathed out, drawing from the pool inside her, spilling it out like she did with the tea.

Instead of dipping into it she plunged in, scooping the longing out in a great splash.

Her hand began to burn, then sear and she dropped the horn onto the chair, cradling her hand against her chest. Across her palm, wide red blisters rose. Wincing, she picked the horn back up and brought it to her lips. Taking a deep breath, she blew and a wavering, low note rang out from it. Not as loud as the first had been. But she'd done it! She had added power to the horn!

Eliese looked from her palm to the horn. Inside her the pool of longing swelled and surged. She felt exhilarated and exhausted. And her hand stung with pain.

Oriana. She needed Oriana.

Eliese took a step toward the door, hope bursting open in her chest. The Keeper could put power into it. More than before. And then the horn would...

Eliese paused. It would do what? The stones around the room hadn't been transformed into an army. The horn had done nothing but blow like a horn. Granted, if a little magic made it that loud, a lot of magic might make it deafening. But Noreth wasn't going to be scared off by a loud noise.

The idea snagged in her mind. A loud noise. The war cries of two young boys had started a rockslide in the gorge. Maybe a deafening horn could do something more. Maybe she could throw a mountain in Noreth's path. She ran toward the door. How many hours until dawn? She'd need at least two. There had to be at least two.

Eliese ran through the keep. The council room was empty and dark, her father's study the same. She ran outside and found the walls lined with men and torches. The sky above twinkled with more stars than seemed possible, and the eastern sky was still black.

Eliese ran up the stairs to the top of the wall, past the watchmen. Through breaks in the parapet she could see the blackness of the gorge. If there was an army there, it was hidden by the shadows.

Halfway around the wall she found Marcus and grabbed his arm. "Keeper Oriana, where is she?"

Marcus looked at her in surprise. "Gone."

Eliese stared at him, her mind trying to wrap itself around the word.

"She left from the council, hoping she could get the reinforcements to send troops faster. She's been gone for hours."

Eliese sank back against the wall. Oriana couldn't be gone. She needed to fill the horn.

"What's wrong, Eliese?"

Eliese explained how Oriana's power had fixed the horn, the words spilling out of her mouth. When she finished, his brow wrinkled and he shook his head. "I don't know, El. The watch blows horns all the time in the gorge and there's never rockslides."

"They never stand were we did," she said. "It's the narrowest, steepest part of the gorge. It echoes and..."

Marcus's face was troubled. "Eliese, I know you've always had a...fascination for that horn, but..."

"You didn't hear it," she insisted. "It's more than a horn."

He looked at her for a long minute. "I believe you," he said finally. "But Oriana is gone. There's no one to put any...whatever into it."

Eliese shifted her grip on the horn and pain lanced across the blisters on her hand. Her hand tightened on it for a moment. "Maybe there is," she said quietly. She told him about putting her own power in.

Marcus's face grew more astonished the more she talked.

"You did it?" he asked.

"Not as loud as she did, and it really hurt." She held out her palm to him. "I guess you are right about my tea."

Marcus held her hand out toward the torchlight and winced. "If a little bit hurt this much, how are you going to put enough in to make it really loud?"

Eliese's will faltered for a moment. Even what Oriana had put in wouldn't be loud enough. The Keeper's words came back to her mind. *If I were to try to fill it, it would kill me.*

But maybe she wouldn't have to fill it. Just put some power in. It would hurt, of course, but she could stop before it killed her.

She needed to go. Turning to Marcus she grabbed his hand. "When do the men go out to fight?"

"Your father plans to take our position in the pass at dawn." His eyes were troubled watching her.

"I can't bear the thought of you all going out," she said. "I can't bear the idea of not knowing what is happening to you."

"Eliese—" he began.

She shook her head. "If I had tea I'd brew it and wish we could know each other were safe. Once we drank it, we'd know if—if anything happened to either of us."

But Oriana had said the magic was in her, not in the tea. Eliese couldn't walk off this wall and not know.

She pulled Marcus's head down until his forehead leaned against hers. "I want to know that you're safe," she whispered, the longing for it rushing up and spilling out of her, flowing into him. "I want us to know that each other are safe."

Without the tea, the desire flowed more freely. She took a deep breath and in her chest she could feel it--she could feel that right now he was safe. Troubled, but safe.

"Can you feel it?" she asked.

He nodded slowly, watching her with a mixture of awe and uncertainty.

She hesitated just a moment before stretching up and kissing him on the cheek. His skin felt warm and he leaned into her. She wanted to stay here forever.

But her fingers were wrapped around the Black Horn and the troops clanked and rustled nearby, preparing for the dawn. She pushed herself away from him.

He looked down at her, his eyes buoyant and fierce, and grinned. "I like how it works when there's no tea."

"I do too," she whispered.

Then, before she lost all courage, she turned and ran.

5

THE BLACK HORN

Eliese scrambled up onto the windowsill of the back watch tower. This side of the keep was the farthest from the road and it pressed up against the steep cliff. Down into the gorge was a sharp drop, and the top of the cliffs still towered high over her head, so it was inaccessible from above and below. But here the thin goat trail wound along the rock face, scratched into the escarpment.

All of the guards were up at the top of the tower, so no one stopped Eliese as she scrambled through the window. It was a long drop to the ground, but she dropped quickly, before she had time to be scared. She hit the ground hard and the horn cracked against the stones of the keep. Her breath caught at the thought of it breaking. There was only a thin sliver of a moon hanging low in the eastern sky so she couldn't see the horn well, but she ran her fingers over the spiraled horn and it felt undamaged.

The trail scratched out ahead of her, barely visible, but the bottom of the gorge was in shadows. Carefully she began down the path. In the steepest places she leaned on the cliff, trying not to think about the drop off next to her feet. Last time she'd carried the horn here she'd imagined herself transformed into one of the battle maidens of old. But she was no such thing. She was just herself. No different than she'd ever been. As common as everyone else and terribly small in the face of the wide world.

We might not be enough, Marcus had said. *But we have to try.*

She focussed on the feeling in her chest of Marcus. He was safe, she was sure of it. But also frightened.

Maybe this is how every brave person felt. Inadequate, but trying anyway.

It felt like hours before she caught sight of the huge boulder they'd dubbed Lookout Rock as children. Her eyes stung from dust and her palms were raw from the rocks when she clambered onto it. She was so tired that if she lay down, she'd fall asleep.

The eastern sky had lightened from black to blue, washing out the stars. She could just make out the outline of the keep. The biting smell of smoke wafted up, lifted high above the ground by a careless breeze. She stepped to the edge of the boulder and looked down. In the pre-dawn light she could finally see the floor of the gorge.

Hordes of Wildmen filled the base of the canyon. Below her, straight down the sheer face, orders rang out and the clumps of men began to shift, organizing themselves into loose lines.

Eliese shrank back from the edge and slipped the horn out of the sling. The sky had bleached to a pale yellow. It was minutes from dawn. Small figures moved along the top of the keep wall, but her father and his men hadn't emerged yet.

She thought of Marcus, preparing with the others to fight and knew deep in her gut that he was safe. For now.

In the pale light the horn looked thinner, less substantial than ever. It looked as though it couldn't hold a cup of water, never mind a well of magic. She held it in trembling hands. The world was lifeless and empty around her, made of nothing but thin morning light.

Closing her eyes, she reached into herself, searching for the pool.

And felt nothing.

Her heart began to pound and her hands felt slippery on the horn. She took a deep breath and focused on her longing.

"I want the keep to be safe," she whispered. And with those words, the flood gates opened. The pool within her surged up, pouring out in a river. Her hands on the horn began to sting, then burn and she almost stopped. But then she pictured the men of the keep, standing ready to sacrifice their own lives to stop the enemy. She gripped the horn harder and dropped to her knees, willing more and more power into it.

Pain seared through her hands and up her arms. She could feel the pool inside her emptying. But the horn wasn't full yet. And then it wasn't just the pool flowing out of her, it was something more intrinsic. An energy that came from her muscles, her bones, her mind. With a cry she dropped the horn, cutting off the horn before it pulled so much out of her she wouldn't even be able to blow it.

When the rush of power had stopped, blood dripped from her palms. She curled forward, crushed by exhaustion and pain. Her body pressed down heavily against the rock. With a monstrous effort, she cracked her eyes open.

A sliver of the sun crested the horizon, lighting the stones around her with deep, rust-red.

Below, the army began to creep forward, and out of the corner of her eye she caught some movement. The gates of Stone Gap cracked open.

The thought of her father and Rellien and Marcus and the men propelled her to her feet.

With fear rising to choke her, Eliese heaved the horn up to her lips and filled it with her anguish and fury. She willed the gorge to fall, willed the rocks to collapse. The note began hollow and haunted. But then it grew, sharp and clear. It cut through the air and her desire sliced through the morning with it. She blew again, a wild blast fierce and free. It echoed off the stone walls of the gorge, crashing against itself. The echoes slammed into each other, swelling rather than fading away until the very earth shook.

The approaching army paused.

And the rock face shifted.

In a breath Eliese crashed to her knees on a promontory, jutting out into a rushing sea of rock. The rock shook and she peered over the edge. The army below scattered and began to run, crashing into each other, crying out as the rocks surged down, filling the gorge between them and the keep, crushing the front lines.

All around her, boulders and stones crashed through a sea of smaller rocks, tumbling down the slope. Rocks raced down the slope above her, smashing into each other before launching out into the gorge. She clawed her way to the cliff wall, as far as she could get from the edge, fighting against the falling rocks and the crushing exhaustion. She curled into a ball, wrapping her arms over her head.

Rocks pelted her from above and beneath her body the boulder groaned and shook. Her hands and arms were on fire with pain, and everything inside of her felt empty. Hollow.

She was terrified for a moment of the pain she knew was coming. When she dared to peek up above her, it was nothing but a waterfall of falling rocks. More and more came until the entire world was a rush of stone, falling to crush her.

Darkness crept in from the corners of her view and she gave in to the merciful exhaustion as everything went black.

EPILOGUE

To: The Shield and all the Keepers at the Stronghold
  From: Keeper Oriana at Stone Gap.

Enclosed is the official record of the events from the last day at Stone Gap. They are momentous for the country and fascinating in their own right. Noreth and the other warlords rode with the advanced guard and all were crushed. The Wildmen are in disarray and leaderless, fleeing back into the wilds. With Noreth dead, perhaps the next leader will be more inclined toward peace.

But in a personal note, I would like to apologize for two misjudgments I made.

The first involves the Black Horn.

I examined it myself before the battle. Eliese had brought it to me in the hopes of finding that it held some great magic that would protect the keep. Although it was ancient and strange, I could sense no power in it. I told her that even if it could be filled, it would be nothing more than a horn.

However, I heard the horn call from a great distance away, and there was...*something* in it, something more than a horn blast.

The legend of the horn claimed it could call forth an army of stone men, and that is essentially what it did. Whether that was coincidental or not, I do not know. If the horn has survived the rockslide, it should be examined more thoroughly.

The other thing I misjudged was Eliese herself. The folks in Stone Gap believed that she had magical skills. If she brewed someone tea, anything she desired while brewing would come to fruition. I think even she had a faltering belief that it was true.

I admit I doubted.

But she made me tea, and wished that I would keep the soldiers of Stone Gap safe. Which is what I intended to do by calling the reinforcements to hurry.

But just after I drank the tea, I also inspected the horn. I put energy into it, just to see if it would hold. It did. The horn seemed almost hungry for it. It was just a little bit of energy and I'd almost forgotten about it. But that power let Eliese know what the horn was capable of. And so it turns out I did help Eliese keep the Gap safe after all.

I do not know what happened to Eliese, but I cannot imagine she survived. Her father sighted her just before she blew the horn, standing on a rock in the center of the widest slide. But both sides of the canyon for two hundred paces has collapsed. The gorge is unrecognizable and utterly blocked.

And beyond the rock slide, the amount of power she must

have poured into the horn to create such a sound--it's a wonder she survived long enough to blow it.

They mourn her in Stone Gap, even as they hail her as a hero. The locals have already written songs about Eliese and the Black Horn, of her magic and her sacrifice.

In truth, not everyone mourns. One man, a lieutenant Marcus, claims he knows she lives. He leads search parties incessantly, scouring the gorge for her. His confidence is unshakable and he insists Eliese "wanted him to know if she was safe."

I've been pondering what sort of spell a bond like that would entail and am having a hard time imagining one. He calls it magic. And it very well might be. But it may just be love.

Either way, I keep being tempted to believe him. After all, I misjudged Eliese before.

So I believe I will remain a few more days, just in case Marcus turns out to be right.

Your servant,
 Oriana

AFTERWORD

Thank you for reading *The Black Horn*.

You can read more about the Keepers and their stories in *The Keeper Chronicles*.

The series begins with *A Threat of Shadows*. You can find it and other books of mine on my website at jaandrews.com.

A THREAT OF SHADOWS

THE KEEPER
CHRONICLES
BOOK 1

If you'd like a quick note when I have new releases out, please sign up for my Bookish Things newsletter. I send short emails a few times a month letting you know about anything new in my own books and any good sales or promotions I come across.

You can find it at www.jaandrews.com.

(Turn to the next page to read chapter one of A Threat of Shadows.)

A THREAT OF SHADOWS - CH 1

The deeper Alaric rode into the woods, the more something felt... off. This forest had always fit like a well-worn cloak. But tonight, the way the forest wrapped around felt familiar, but not quite comfortable, as though it remembered wrapping around a slightly different shape.

"This path used to be easier to follow," Alaric said to his horse, Beast, as they paused between patches of summer moonlight. Alaric peered ahead, looking for the trail leading to the Stronghold. He found it running like a scratch through the low brush to the right. "If the Keepers weren't too meek to hold grudges, I'd think the old men were hiding it from me."

All the usual smells of pine and moss and dirt wove through the air, the usual sounds of little animals going about their lives, but Alaric kept catching a hint of something different. Something more complicated than he wanted to deal with.

Around the next turn, the trail ran straight into a wide tree trunk. Alaric leaned as far to the side as he could, but he couldn't see around it. "I could be wrong about the Keepers holding grudges."

Well, if they didn't want him at the Stronghold, that was too bad. He didn't need a warm welcome. He just needed to find one book with one antidote. With a little luck, the book would be easy to find and he could leave quickly. With a lot of luck, he'd get in and out without having to answer anyone's questions about what he'd been doing for the past year.

Beast circled the tree and found the path again, snaking out the other side. As his hooves thudded down on it, a howl echoed through the woods.

The horse froze, and Alaric grabbed the pouch hanging around his neck, protecting it against his chest. He closed his eyes, casting out past the nearest trees and through the woods, searching for the blazing energy of the wolf. He sensed nothing beyond the tranquil glow of the trees and the dashing flashes of frightened rabbits.

"That's new." Alaric opened his eyes and peered into the darkness.

A louder howl broke through the night. Beast shuddered.

"It's all right." Alaric patted Beast's neck as he cast farther out. The life energy of an animal as large as a wolf would be like a bonfire among the trees, but there was nothing near them. "It's not wolves. Just disembodied howls." He kept his voice soothing, hoping to calm the animal.

"That didn't sound as reassuring as I meant it to. But a real wolf pack wouldn't keep howling as they got closer. If we were being tracked by wolves, we wouldn't know it."

Beast's ears flicked back and forth, alert for another howl.

"Okay, that wasn't reassuring, either." Alaric nudged him forward. "C'mon we're almost to the Wall."

A third howl tore out of the darkness right beside them.

Beast reared back, whinnying in terror. Alaric grabbed for the saddle and swore. He pressed his hand to Beast's neck.

"*Paxa*," he said, focusing energy through his hand and into Beast. A shock of pain raced across Alaric's palm where it touched the horse, as the energy rushed through.

Mid-snort, Beast settled and stood still.

Alaric shook out his hand and looked thoughtfully into the woods. This wasn't about a grudge, or at least the howls weren't directed at him. Any Keeper would know there were no wolves. Even one as inadequate as he would know there was no energy, no *vitalle*, behind the sounds. So what was the purpose of it? The path had never been like this before.

With Beast calm, Alaric set him back into a steady walk. Two more howls rang out from the woods, but Beast ambled along, unruffled. Alaric rubbed his still-tingling palm.

Beast paused again as the trail ran into another wide tree.

Alaric growled in frustration. The path to the Keepers' Stronghold shouldn't be this troublesome for a Keeper.

Unless it no longer recognized him as one. That was a sobering thought.

As they skirted around the tree, a white face thrust itself out of the trunk. Alaric jerked away as the hazy form of a man leaned out toward him. When the figure didn't move, Alaric reined in Beast and forced himself to study it. It held no life energy, it was just an illusion—like the wolves.

The figure was a young man. He had faded yellow hair and milky white skin. Once the initial shock wore off, the man was not particularly frightening.

"What are you supposed be? A friendly ghost?" Alaric asked.

It hung silent on the tree. Alaric leaned forward and backward, but the ghost remained still, staring off into the woods.

"The howls were more frightening than you." Alaric set Beast to walking again.

"You are lost," the ghost whispered as he passed.

Alaric gave a short laugh. "I've been lost many times in my life, but this isn't one of them. And if it's your job to scare people off, you should consider saying something more chilling and less...depressing."

Beast kept walking, and Alaric turned to watch the ghost fade into the darkness behind them.

A rasp pulled his attention forward. Another white form slid out of the tree they were approaching. This one was a young woman. She was rather pretty, for a ghost.

"Hello." Alaric gave her a polite nod.

"You have failed," she whispered. "You have failed everyone."

Alaric scowled. The words rang uncomfortably true.

Alaric stopped Beast in front of the ghost. Behind the woman's face, Alaric saw thin, silver runes carved on the bark. He couldn't read them through the ghost, but he didn't need to. Narrowing his focus, he cast out ahead of them along the trail, brushing against the trunks with his senses. Now that he knew what he was looking for, he felt the subtle humming runes dotting the trees ahead.

Alaric sat back in the saddle. This wasn't what he expected from the Keepers. The old men protected their privacy like paranoid hermits, but they'd never tried to scare people away before. Of course, these ghosts weren't frightening. If the Keepers were going to make ghosts, these are the kind they would make.

Years ago, during his "Defeat by Demoralization" lesson, Keeper Gerone had declared, "Control the emotions, control the man!" Gerone was probably responsible for the depressing ghosts.

The ghost runes were on almost every tree now, faces appearing every few steps.

"Your powers are worthless," the next whispered and Alaric flinched.

"It's your fault," another rasped. "All your fault."

Alaric clenched his jaw and stared ahead as the whispers surrounded him.

When he passed close to one large tree, a ghost thrust out close to him. Alaric turned toward it and saw his own face looking back at him. A pale, wasted version of himself. His black hair was faded to a lifeless grey, and his skin, far from being tanned from traveling, was bleached a wrinkly bone white. Only his eyes had stayed dark, sinking from a healthy brown to deep, black pits.

Alaric stared, repulsed, at the withered apparition of himself—it was decades older than his forty years. The ghost looked tired, a deep crease furrowed between its brows. Alaric reached up and rubbed his own forehead.

The ghost leaned closer.

"She's dead," it whispered.

Guilt stabbed into him, deep and familiar. He shuddered, grabbing the pouch at his neck, his mind flooded with the image of Evangeline's sunken face.

Alaric slammed his palm against the rune on the trunk.

"*Uro!*" Pain raced through his hand again. He poured energy into the tree, willing it to burn. The bark smoked as he seared the rune off.

Out of the corner of his eye, pulses of white light appeared along the path ahead of them. He glanced at them, but the distraction had consequences, and the pain flared, arcing up each finger. He gasped and narrowed his focus back to the energy flowing through his palm. The pain receded slightly. The ghost stared a moment longer, then faded away. Alaric dropped his arm, leaving a hand-shaped scorch mark on the trunk where the rune had been.

"She's dead."

Alaric's head snapped forward.

The trees ahead of him were full of ghosts, each a washed-out version of himself.

"Dead… She's dead… Dead." The words filled the air.

Alaric clutched the pouch at his neck until he felt the rough stone inside.

A ghost reached toward him. "She's dead…" Its voice rattled in a long sigh.

Alaric spurred Beast into a gallop, trusting the horse to follow the trail. The whispers clung to them as they ran. Alaric shrank down, hunching his shoulders, wresting his mind away from the memory of his wife's tired eyes, her pale skin.

The trees ended, and they raced out into a silent swath of grass, running up to the base of an immense cliff. Alaric pulled Beast to a stop, both of them breathing hard. Gripping the saddle, Alaric looked back into the trees. The forest was dark and quiet.

"I take it back," he said, catching his breath, "the ghosts were worse than the wolves." He sat in the saddle, pushing back the dread that was enveloping him. She wasn't dead. The ghosts were just illusions. He'd get the antidote tonight. She'd be fine.

When his heart finally slowed, he gave Beast an exhausted pat on the neck.

"This path used to be a *lot* easier to follow."

(If you'd like to continue reading *A Threat of Shadows,* you can find it on Amazon)

ABOUT THE AUTHOR

JA Andrews is a writer, wife, mother, and unemployed rocket scientist. She doesn't regret the rocket science degree, but finds it generally inapplicable in daily life. Except for the rare occurrence of her being able to definitively state, "That's not rocket science." She does, however, love the stars.

She spends an inordinate amount of time at home, with her family, who she adores, and lives deep in the Rocky Mountains of Montana, where she can see more stars than she ever imagined.

For more information, find JA Andrews at:
www.jaandrews.com
jaandrews@jaandrews.com

Made in United States
Orlando, FL
06 November 2024